Tombliboo trousers
on the Ninky Nonk!

Andrew Davenport

Once upon a time in the Night Garden...

The Ninky Nonk came to play.

Igglepiggle, iggle onk,
We're going to catch...

The Ninky Nonk!
Everybody loves the Ninky Nonk!

Here comes the Ninky Nonk.
All aboard the Ninky Nonk!

Tombliboo!

Makka Pakka!

Hello Tombliboos!
Hello Makka Pakka!

The Ninky Nonk went
all over the Garden.

Up a tree,

upside down,

along a branch...

and down the tree again. What a silly Ninky Nonk.

Tombliboo!

Hold on to your trousers, Tombliboos!

At last the Ninky Nonk stopped.

Bye-bye, Makka Pakka!
Bye-bye, Ninky Nonk!

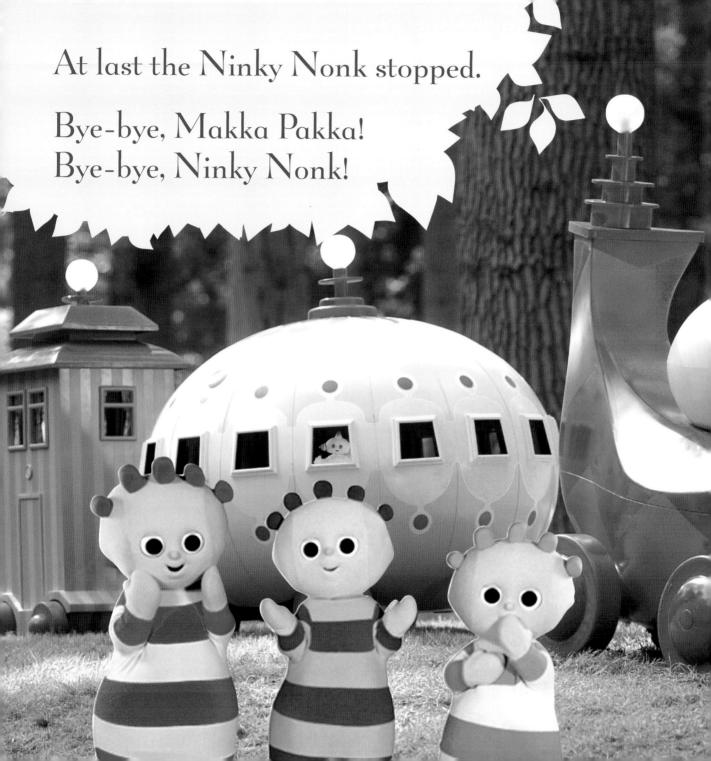

Wait a minute,
Tombliboos –
where are your
Tombliboo trousers?

The Tombliboos
had left their trousers
on the Ninky Nonk!

Catch the Ninky Nonk,
Tombliboos!

Tombliboo!

But the Tombliboos couldn't catch the Ninky Nonk. They had to go home without their Tombliboo trousers.

Poor Tombliboos.

Tombliboo!

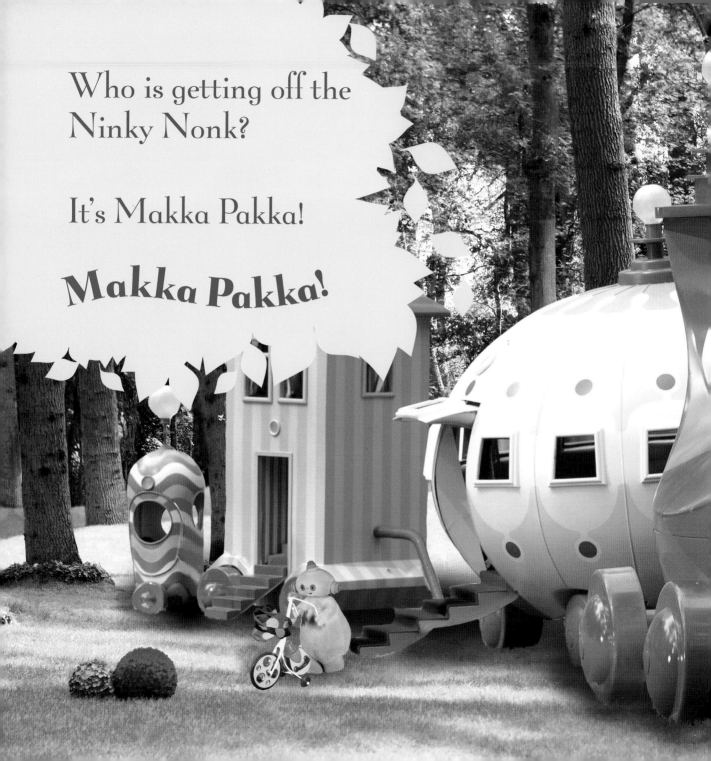

Who is getting off the
Ninky Nonk?

It's Makka Pakka!

Makka Pakka!

Where is Makka Pakka going?

What is Makka Pakka carrying on his Og-pog?

Makka Pakka carried the Tombliboo trousers all the way back to the Tombliboo bush.

Makka Pakka!

Makka Pakka blew his trumpet.

Parp-parp!

The Tombliboos looked out of the windows.

Tombliboo!

The Tombliboos were very pleased to see
Makka Pakka...

Makka
Pakka!

Tombliboo!

and very happy to see their trousers.

One, two, three happy Tombliboos.

Tombliboo!

Thank you, Makka Pakka.

The Tombliboos love their
Tombliboo trousers.

Tombliboo!

The Tombliboos love Makka Pakka.

Makka Pakka!

Makka Pakka loves the Tombliboos...

and everybody loves the Ninky Nonk.

Isn't that a pip?

Once upon a time,
in the Night Garden,

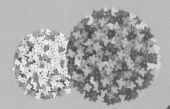

the Tombliboos and Makka Pakka
went for a bouncy ride.

Oh dear, Tombliboos.
Where are your
Tombliboo trousers?

Makka Pakka brought the Tombliboo trousers all the way back to the Tombliboo washing line.

Thank you, Makka Pakka.

Time to go to sleep everybody.

Go to sleep, Tombliboos.

Go to sleep, Makka Pakka.

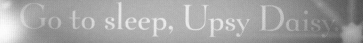

Go to sleep, Upsy Daisy.

Go to sleep, Pontipines.

Go to sleep, Haahoos.

Go to sleep Ninky Nonk
and go to sleep, Pinky Ponk.

Wait a minute.
Somebody is not in bed!
Who's not in bed?
Igglepiggle is not in bed!

Don't worry, Igglepiggle...
it's time to go.